The Wonderful World of Disney

Walt Disney

DUMBO

Twin Books

DERRYDALE BOOKS
New York

On the first day of spring, all the circus animals looked up to
the sky with great hope. The storks were coming! They soon
arrived, and three little bundles were parachuted to the ground.
Out of them came a baby tiger, a bear cub, and a baby giraffe.
But there was no baby elephant for Mrs Jumbo.

"Maybe my stork is late," she thought, but she couldn't wait for it because the circus was going to a new place, and all the animals had to board the train immediately.

Mrs Jumbo was very sad. But then, all of a sudden, she heard a tap on the roof of the train car. A stork, carrying a heavy bundle, slipped in through the air vent.

"Are you Mrs Jumbo, Ma'am?" he asked. "I have a baby elephant for you."

"Oh, isn't he adorable?" cried Mrs Jumbo when the bundle was untied. "I'm so happy to be his mother!"

The other elephants thought the baby elephant adorable too. They envied Mrs Jumbo. But just then, the little elephant sneezed. To everyone's surprise, his two ears flapped out. They were enormous!

"But he's not an elephant," laughed the elephants. "He's more like a bat! Look at his ears!"

The elephants roared with laughter. They pulled and tugged at the enormous ears, and teased the little elephant until he started to cry. He was hurt that they were making fun of him.

"Don't cry, sweetheart!" said Mrs Jumbo. "Please don't cry! You're the handsomest son a mother could want! I love you just the way you are. I've even thought of a name for you. I'm going to call you...Dumbo!"

The little elephant hugged his mother and happily fell asleep.

That very night, the train arrived at its new destination. The circus tent had to be put up by morning, and everyone was put to work, even though it was raining. Dumbo didn't care, because tomorrow there'd be the parade. He pictured himself walking proudly behind his mother. How much fun it would be! He grabbed hold of his mother's tail and happily followed her as she worked.

The parade was a great success.
Everybody clapped very hard as Dumbo
walked by. He beamed with pleasure.

But the other elephants ignored him. They were very angry that he had stolen the show. Out of spite, they had his mother locked up.

Poor Dumbo was miserable. He missed his mother very much, and could not understand why the elephants were so mean.

All of a sudden, a little mouse appeared.

"Hi, I'm Timothy," he announced. "You look pretty sad, kid. Can I help?"

Dumbo didn't know how the mouse could help, but Timothy was optimistic. "I've got plans for you, Dumbo," he said. "You're going to be a star! Then the ringmaster will have to free your mother."

Dumbo was thrilled. He grabbed hold
of Timothy's tail and followed him around.

That night, when everyone was asleep, Timothy slipped into the ringmaster's tent. The ringmaster was sound asleep, snoring loudly. Quickly, the little mouse whispered into his ear an idea for a new act for Dumbo.

The following morning, the ringmaster woke up with a wonderful idea in his head.

The ringmaster wasted
little time. The following
night the new act opened.
"Ladies and Gentlemen,
let me introduce our next
act, an act of courage, an
act of audacity, an act you
will see only here, the best
act in the history of the
circus!"

The drums rolled in anticipation. The largest of the elephants stepped into the ring and climbed on top of a large ball.

A second elephant followed and climbed on top of the first, and a third on top of the second, until...

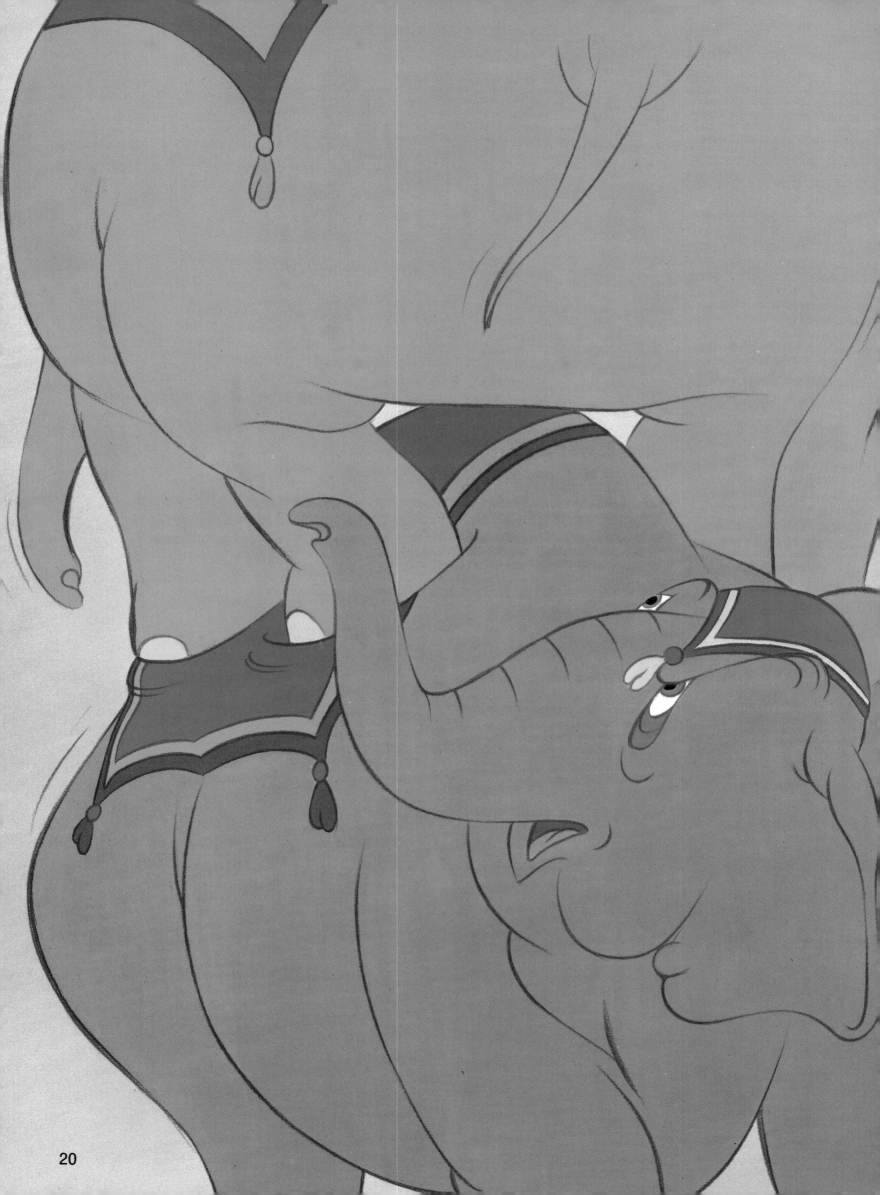

...all the elephants stood on top of one another, forming a giant tower of elephants.

"Take your foot out of my eye!" grumbled the elephant at the very bottom.

"Quiet! Listen to the ringmaster," whispered another one.

The drums rolled again and the ringmaster's voice boomed across the circus tent.

"Ladies and Gentlemen, hold your breath for you will not believe what you will see! Dumbo will jump from a springboard to the very top of the tower!"

The curtain was drawn and Dumbo appeared. Timothy had carefully tied his ears together so they would not get in the way and ruin the act.

"One, two, and three!" Dumbo leaped onto the springboard, but his ears came untied. He tripped and was catapulted right into the ball that held up all the elephants.

One by one, the elephants tumbled to
the ground, while the audience screamed
with fear. Panic filled the circus tent.

Then, with a loud crack, the circus tent caved in and collapsed on top of everyone. Screams and shouts were heard everywhere.

Poor Dumbo! It seemed his new act was a flop.

All the other elephants were badly bruised and scratched.
Some had bumps on their heads and others had black eyes.

"Look at us!" they cried. "That little idiot almost killed us! He spoiled our chance at success, and humiliated us in front of our public! We must do something about this!"

They decided that the ringmaster should lock up Dumbo.

"That way, he'll be with his mother!" they added meanly.

But the ringmaster had other plans for Dumbo. "This little elephant may be clumsy, but he'd make an excellent clown!" he mused.

He dressed Dumbo up as a baby with a bonnet, and had him climb to the top of a house for the new act.

The house seemed to be on fire. While one clown, dressed as Dumbo's mother, screamed for help, the other clowns, dressed as firemen, pretended to put the fire out. Then Dumbo was supposed to jump into a net.

Dumbo was terrified, but
he had to jump. He held
his breath and stepped off
the platform.

He dropped down like a sack of stones. Instead of bouncing off the safety net, he crashed right through it...

...and landed in an enormous tub filled with soap suds!

The audience roared with laughter and applause. The new act was a hit. The clowns were happy and celebrated their success, but Dumbo went straight to bed, hoping to forget his troubles. Timothy comforted him and soon the little elephant was asleep.

But then, when Timothy
had fallen asleep too,
Dumbo dreamt that he
floated up towards the sky....

The following morning, Dumbo and Timothy were sound asleep on a branch up in a tree. A flock of crows spotted them. "How on earth did they get here?" mused one of the crows. "Elephants can't fly!"

"They sure can't," agreed another. "We'd better go ask them!"
They flew over to the branch and woke up Dumbo and
Timothy. Dumbo and Timothy were just as surprised as the
crows. They couldn't think of anything to say.

When they were safely on the ground again, Timothy tried to figure out how they had ended up in the tree.

"The only thing I remember," he said to Dumbo, "was a strange dream I had. I dreamt that we were flying!"

"Mmm.... Maybe it wasn't a dream.... Maybe you did fly! Your ears are so big that they look like wings!" said Timothy, thoughtfully.

"The only way we can know for sure is to try," decided Timothy. He called the crows over. They led Dumbo to a ledge. From there he could jump off and fly. To give him faith, the crows offered Dumbo a 'magic' feather. Then they gave him a push and seconds later, the little elephant was flying!

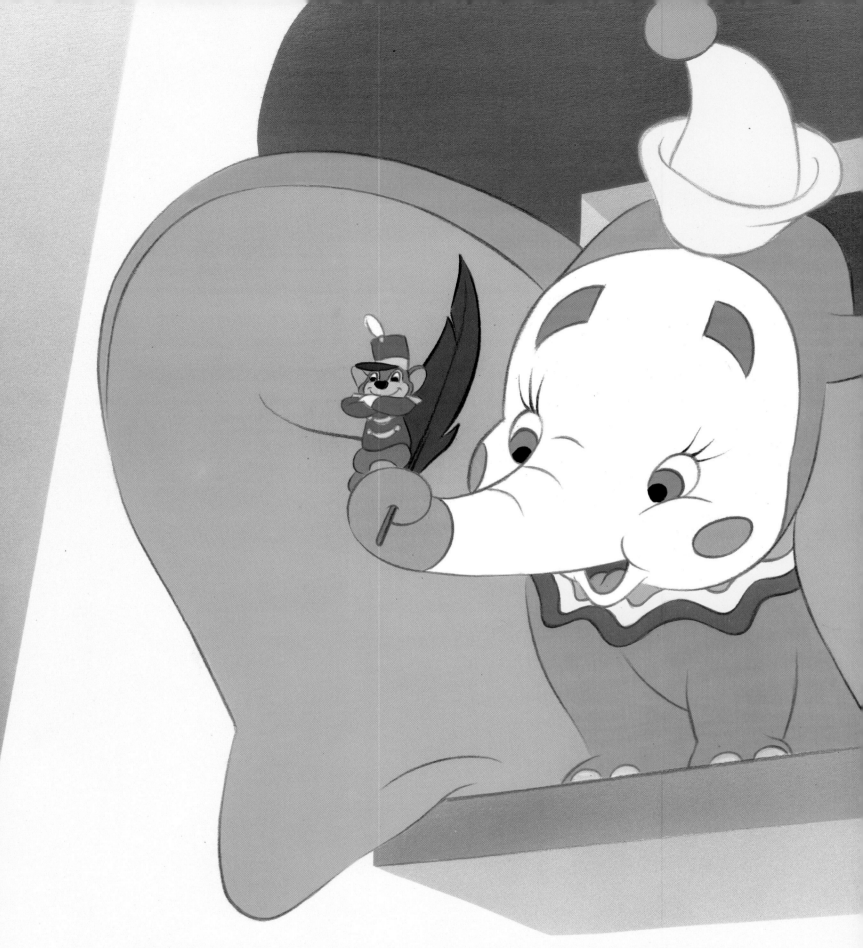

That night, before they entered the circus ring Timothy slipped into Dumbo's hat. He had made sure that Dumbo was holding his 'magic' feather. The ringmaster had ordered the house to be twice as high because the act had been so successful the night before.

But when it was time to jump, Dumbo was not afraid. Instead, he winked at his friend Timothy.

He spread his ears and gracefully jumped off the platform. The audience stopped laughing. They couldn't believe their eyes. Instead of falling, the little elephant glided up into the air. The clowns, too, were amazed.

But all fo a sudden, the 'magic' feather slipped from Dumbo's grasp. Dumbo panicked and stopped flapping his ears.

He started to fall, but Timothy screamed, "Dumbo! You can fly without the 'magic' feather! You did it that night, remember?"

Dumbo came to his senses just in time.
Within inches of the safety net, he
flapped his ears and flew away. The
audience cheered with delight.

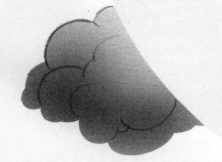

Mrs Jumbo was freed that very night. After all, her son was the star of the circus! She was very proud of him.

Even the other elephants were proud of
Dumbo the Flying Elephant!

Mrs Jumbo was the happiest elephant in the circus. Her darling Dumbo was a star, and she was very proud.

Timothy was proud of Dumbo, too, for the little elephant had proved that he had both courage and self-confidence. Together they made a terrific team, and Dumbo the Flying Elephant quickly became one of the most successful acts in the history of the circus.

This 1988 edition published by Derrydale Books, distributed by Crown Publishers, Inc., 225 Park Avenue South New York, New York 10003

Produced by Twin Books
15 Sherwood Place
Greenwich, CT 06830

Directed by HELENA Productions Ltd

Image adaption by Van Gool-Lefevre-Loiseaux

Printed and bound in Hong Kong

ISBN 0-517-66197-7

hgfedcba